Give Maggie
a Chance

Design by Wycliffe Smith

Published in Canada by Fitzhenry & Whiteside, 195 Allstate Parkway, Markham, Ontario L3R 4T8

Published in the United States by Fitzhenry & Whiteside, 121 Harvard Avenue, Suite 2, Allston, Massachusetts 02134

www.fitzhenry.ca   godwit@fitzhenry.ca.

10 9 8 7 6 5 4 3 2 1

National Library of Canada Cataloguing in Publication Data

Wishinsky, Frieda
Give Maggie a Chance

ISBN 1-55041-682-0 (bound) ISBN 1-55041-730-4 (pbk.)

I. Griffiths, Dean, 1967- II. Title.

PS8595.I834G58 2002   jC813'.54   C2002-900335-0
PZ7.W78032Gi 2002

U.S. Publisher Cataloging-in-Publication Data
(Library of Congress Standards)

Wishinsky, Frieda.
Give Maggie a chance / written by Frieda Wishinsky ; illustrated by Dean Griffiths. -- 1st ed.
[32] p. : col. ill. ; cm.
Summary: When push comes to shove, timid Maggie is determined to overcome
her catty rival and not be intimidated.

ISBN 1-55041-682-0
ISBN 1-55041-730-4 (pbk)
1. Fear -- Fiction. 2. Teasing -- Fiction. 3. Courage -- Fiction. I. Griffiths, Dean, ill. II. Title.
[E] 21 2002 AC CIP

Fitzhenry & Whiteside acknowledges with thanks the Canada Council for the Arts, the Government of
Canada through the Book Publishing Industry Development Program (BPIDP), and the Ontario Arts
Council for their support for our publishing program.

Give Maggie
a Chance

by Frieda Wishinsky

Illustrated by Dean Griffiths

Fitzhenry & Whiteside

For my friend, Deborah Braithwaite.
Frieda

To Ann for her kindness, friendship, wisdom,
and making sure my cats don't
look like ferrets.
Dean

Maggie leaped out of bed. She
slipped on her new dress and spun
like a ballerina in her new shoes.

She skipped all the way to her new class.

At school, Maggie sat in the second row beside Sam.
Kimberly sat in front of them.

The teacher, Mrs. Brown, said, "Who
would like to come up
and read?"

Maggie's hand shot up.
She was good at reading.

Maggie walked to the front of the class.
Her heart thumped like a drum.
Her knees quivered like jelly.
Her mouth felt as dry as a desert.

Maggie opened her mouth
but nothing came out.
Not a word. Not a sound.
Not even a whisper.

"Let me read! Let me read!" shouted
Kimberly, leaping out
of her seat.

"Sit down, Kimberly," said
Mrs. Brown. "Give
Maggie a chance."

But Maggie didn't want
a chance.

Maggie wanted the floor to swallow her up.

Maggie wanted a rocket to blast her to Mars.

Maggie wanted a genie to make the class disappear.

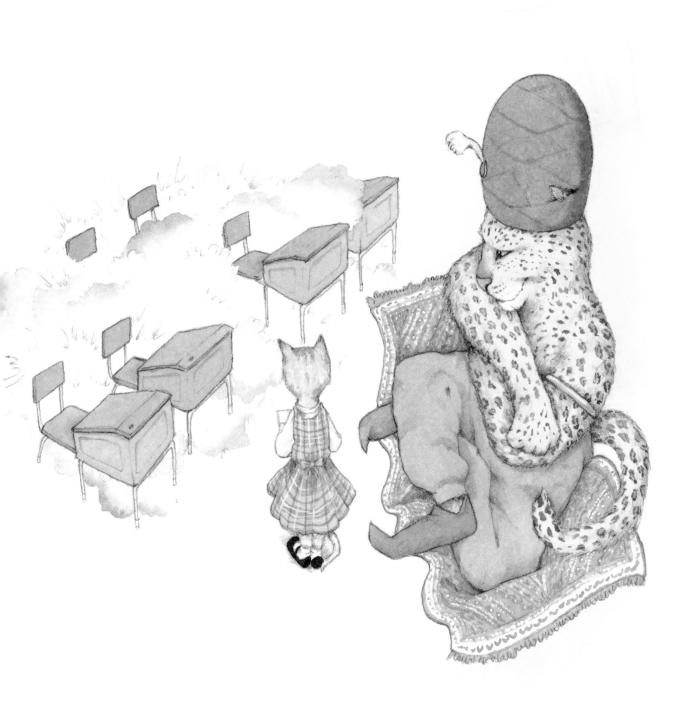

But the class did not disappear
and Kimberly read.

The day dragged on. Like a nightmare, it wouldn't end.

Finally the home bell rang.

Kimberly tapped Maggie on the shoulder. "Reading is SO easy," said Kimberly.
"I've been reading since I was a baby."

Maggie's face turned as red as a radish.

"D...D... Don't," said Sam. "D...Don't let Kimberly bother you."

"I'll try," said Maggie. But it was hard.

Maggie trudged home.

"How was school today?" asked her mother.

"Terrible," said Maggie.

"Maybe tomorrow will be better," said her mother.

"Maybe tomorrow will be worse," said Maggie.

At home, Maggie slumped on her bed. She felt like crying.

Then she remembered Sam's words. Sam was right!
She shouldn't let Kimberly bother her.

Maggie stood up.

She lined her stuffed animals on her bed. She read
them a story loudly, clearly, perfectly.
Just like a teacher.

"Tomorrow I'll read like that to my class," she told herself.

The next day, Mrs. Brown said,
"Who'll read the first line in our
new book?"

Maggie's hand shot up.

"Maggie," said Mrs. Brown. Maggie
opened her mouth to read.
But nothing came out.

The teacher waited. The class waited.

Everyone waited—except Kimberly.

"My turn. My turn," called Kimberly,
jumping up and down like a yo-yo.

"Maggie, you'll read another time,"
said Mrs. Brown gently. "Go
ahead, Kimberly."

Maggie wished a giant wave would wash
Kimberly out the door.

She wished a giant bird would fly
Kimberly out the window.

She wished a giant troll would dump
Kimberly into a dungeon.

But a wave didn't come. A bird didn't fly.
A troll didn't show.

Kimberly read.

The day dragged on. Like a toothache it wouldn't end.

Finally the home bell rang.

Kimberly tapped Maggie on the shoulder. "The last book I read had one hundred pages and a million hard words," she said.

Maggie's eyes flooded with tears.

"D...D...Don't worry," stuttered Sam. "You'll
read tomorrow."

Maggie brushed her tears away.
"I hope so," she said.

All the way home, Maggie remembered Sam's words.
"I'll read tomorrow," she promised herself. "I won't
let anything stop me."

The next day Mrs. Brown asked,
"Who'd like to read problem
number three in our math book?"

Maggie took a deep breath. Today
was the day. Today she'd read.
All she had to do was raise her hand.

But Maggie couldn't move her hand. Her hands felt
glued to her sides.

Maggie's heart sunk as Kimberly flapped her hands
in the air like a seagull.

"Me! Me!" shouted
Kimberly.

Mrs. Brown called on Sam.
"It's ss...ss...ss..." stuttered Sam.
Mrs. Brown waited. "Sss...sss..."
Sam tried again.

"What's the matter with you?"
snickered Kimberly. "Can't
you talk?"

Sam sunk down in his chair.

Maggie couldn't stand it. She glared at Kimberly.
"Give Sam a chance," said Maggie. "Sam knows the answer."

"But he can't say it," sneered Kimberly.

"Oh, yes he can," said Maggie.

"Sss…six!" said Sam, popping out of his seat.

"Right, Sam!" said Mrs. Brown. "Now, who'd
like to come up and explain the problem
to the class?"

Maggie's hand shot up.

"Come on up, Maggie," said Mrs. Brown.

Maggie walked to the front of the class.
And as she did, Kimberly made a rude noise
and stuck out her tongue.

But Maggie didn't care what Kimberly did.
Maggie didn't care what Kimberly thought.

It was as if a magician had whisked Kimberly away.

It was as if a witch had poofed her to smoke.

It was as if a wizard had turned her
into a small, warty toad.

Maggie only saw her friend Sam. Sam was smiling at her.

Sam knew Maggie could do it. Sam knew
Maggie didn't need any more chances.
Sam knew that today Maggie would read
in front of the class.

So she did.